For Jack
~NG

For Granny & Grandad
~VC

LITTLE TIGER PRESS
An imprint of Magi Publications
1 The Coda Centre, Munster Road, London SW6 6AW
First published in Great Britain 2000
Text © 2000 Nigel Gray
Illustrations © 2000 Vanessa Cabban
Nigel Gray and Vanessa Cabban have asserted their rights
to be identified as the author and illustrator of this work
under the Copyright, Designs and Patents Act, 1988.
Printed in Belgium by Proost NV, Turnhout
All rights reserved
ISBN 1 85430 636 7
1 3 5 7 9 10 8 6 4 2

Little Bear's Grandad

by NIGEL GRAY

Illustrated by VANESSA CABBAN

LITTLE TIGER PRESS

London

Every Friday Little Bear went to see his grandad.
"How's my favourite little bear?" Grandad
always asked.

"Good," said Little Bear. "And how is my
favourite grandad?"
"Just as good as an old grandad could be,"
Grandad replied.

Every Friday they had tea together, and Little Bear
looked out of the window at Grandad's garden.
In the garden was a very big, very old tree.
And in the tree was a wonky platform which
Grandad called the Tree House.

And so that Grandad and Little Bear could climb up to the Tree House, Grandad kept a ladder leaning there.

After tea Grandad and Little Bear always
climbed up into the Tree House and, sitting
side by side, looked out at the world.
"Life is a gift, Little Bear," Grandad said.
"Don't waste it."
And Little Bear replied, "I'll try not to,
Grandad. I'll do my best."
"Doing your best is the best any
bear can do," said Grandad.

From the Tree House they
could see Grandad's garden
which was green and
overgrown. Grandad called
it the Jungle.

They could see a grassy hill with three grey boulders on top. Grandad called it the Three Bears Hill.

They could see a river which squiggled and squirmed through the valley and changed colour with the weather. At sunset it sometimes looked golden and Grandad called it the Goldilocks River.

They could see an old factory chimney. Grandad had worked in that factory when he was young. He called it the Factory of Lost Youth. But no smoke came from that chimney any more.

Grandad and Little Bear climbed up into the Tree House when it was sunny . . .

and when it was windy . . .

and when it rained – as long as it didn't rain *too* hard.

They even went there when
snow lay on the ground.
They took cardboard
to sit on—but they
never stayed
too long.

And every Friday, as they sat comfortably on the platform in the tree, Little Bear said, "Tell me a story, Grandad."
And Grandad told stories of when he was young.
And Little Bear listened and was just as happy as he could be.

But one Friday Little Bear went to see Grandad and
Grandad said, "I'm sorry, Little Bear. I can't come out today."
Grandad sat in his chair and Little Bear perched on the arm,
and Grandad told Little Bear a story about when he had
been just a little bear himself.

The following Friday Little Bear didn't go to Grandad's
house. Instead, Little Bear's mother took him to the
hospital. There he found Grandad lying in bed.
"You're lazy, Grandad," said Little Bear.
"I *am* lazy," said Grandad. "I haven't got up all day."

Little Bear's mum went to talk to the doctor while Little Bear sat on Grandad's bed and held his paw.

"Tell me a story, Grandad," said Little Bear.

"I'm sorry, I'm too tired," Grandad said. "Why don't you tell *me* a story instead."

So Little Bear told a story about a little bear who went to visit his grandad every Friday, and how they always climbed into a tree house in Grandad's garden. And he described to Grandad all the things they could see.

When he had finished his story, Little Bear asked,
"Did you like that story, Grandad?"
But Grandad didn't reply.
Little Bear's mother came, and she called a nurse.
And the nurse called a doctor.

Then Little Bear's mother told Little Bear that Grandad
had fallen into the very deepest of deep, deep sleeps.
"When will he wake up?" asked Little Bear.
Little Bear's mother put her arms around Little Bear
and held him tight.
"He won't wake up," she said.

Little Bear and his mother
went back to Grandad's house.

They climbed the ladder on to
the wonky platform in the tree.

They sat together, and cried quietly,
and hugged each other, looking out at
the well-known things they could see.

Then, between sobs and snuffles,
Little Bear said, "When I'm a
grandad, I want to be as
nice a grandad as my
grandad was to me."

"You will be, Little Bear,"
his mother said. "You will be."

Can we play too, Piglittle?

Sally Grindley • Andy Ellis

little ORCHARD

One day Piglittle found a ball near the pigsty and began to play with it.

"Can we play with it too?"
asked Peony and Podge.
"No," said Piglittle. "It's mine."

Piglittle pushed the ball with his nose and then chased after it.

"I'm coming to get you," he squealed each time, but the ball never rolled very far away.

He found a bucket and a large pear,
and kicked the ball between them.

"GOAL!" he squealed. "GOAL! GOAL!"
But it was no fun playing alone.

"Shall I be goalie?" asked
Shoo Sheepdog.
"Yes, please," said Piglittle.

But Shoo Sheepdog was so good that Piglittle couldn't score a goal, however hard he tried.

"This ball is no fun,"
muttered Piglittle.

He kicked it as hard as he could into the bushes.

Soon after, Peony and Podge
found the ball.

They played catch and kicked it to each other and took it in turns to be goalie.

When Piglittle saw them, he ran to his mum and whimpered, "They've taken my ball."

"Why don't you all play with it together, my poppet," said Primrose Pig.

"Please can I play with you?" squealed Piglittle.

"Of course," said Peony.

"Let's play piggy-in-the-middle," said Podge.